A CABIN IN CRIPPLE CREEK

BY SUE LUXA

WESTERN REFLECTIONS
PUBLISHING COMPANY®

Montrose, Colorado

ISBN 1-932738-04-5
Library of Congress Control Number: 2004100358

First Edition
Printed in the United States of America

Cover illustration © 2004 by Joyce M. Turley,
  Dixon Cove Design
Cover and text design by Laurie Goralka Design

Western Reflections Publishing Company®
219 Main Street
Montrose, CO 81401
www.westernreflectionspub.com

For Leila, who lived it.

TABLE OF CONTENTS

Chapter 1
THE GRAND ADVENTURE BEGINS

It was going to be a grand adventure! Ten-year-old Mary Haskins was sure of that as she bumped along the rutted road in Papa's rented buckboard wagon. The Haskins family was off to join the gold rushers headed for Cripple Creek, Colorado. The year was 1895, and the rush had been on since 1891.

In the back of the wagon were as many possessions as Papa could cram in. Mama had insisted on taking her lace curtains because it was her belief that no house could be a home without them. The curtains had adorned their home in Denver, and they would be a piece of home in an uncultivated city. There was also Grandma Haskins' marble-topped, spindly-legged table that Mama treasured as part of Papa's family. Oh, yes, and they couldn't forget the red velvet rocking chair! It was interesting how the family's belongings became more important when they were moving to unfamiliar territory. Maybe it was much like the security blanket Mary's three-year-old brother Jacob still took to bed.

Of course, there was also Mama's treadle sewing machine. Mary had watched her Mama sewing clothes for the family, and curtains for the windows and had marveled at her ability to sew a straight seam so effortlessly. The test of an accomplished seamstress was the even, up-and-down foot motion on the treadle below. As far as Mary was concerned, Mama was the best seamstress of all.

Papa had wanted to take lots more, but there just wasn't room. The family had to leave a lot of possessions in Denver because there was only room in the rickety buckboard for the necessary items. Mary would miss her spindle bed. She had hated leaving that most of all. Leaving civilization had been hard for everyone except Papa. The gold fever was strong in his blood, and he just had to find riches in the mountains of Colorado.

Right now, Mary couldn't be sure if the glistening blue sky and the pungent smell of pine trees could make up for the bumpy narrow road. Her rear end was beginning to feel the effects of the constant up-and-down movement. Even the old mules seemed weary. Papa had always said that mules had minds of their own when it came to carrying heavy loads. Why, she had heard stories of mules that just stopped dead in their tracks and wouldn't move no matter how much a person would talk. Even the sharp crack of a whip wouldn't budge those stubborn animals. Luckily, they had experienced no problems with their mules. Perhaps the mules were as eager as the Haskins to reach Cripple Creek. Maybe they were thinking about the hay and oats at the end of the journey.

"Papa, how much farther to Cripple Creek?" whined little Jacob. He was the restless one, fidgeting next to Mama.

"Not too far, son, just around the bend."

Mary doubted that Cripple Creek was just around the bend. Somehow she was expecting a city paved in gold with twinkling gems lying by the side of the road. There would be riches for everyone. Why, they would be able to buy a piano and have the fanciest four-poster bed in all of Colorado when Papa struck it rich in the gold fields.

Papa had told stories and written letters about the new gold-mining camp near Colorado Springs. Once that old rancher, Bob Womack, had come to Denver with his tales of gold and wealth, the march had been on. Single men and men with families had put together their supplies and hurried off to strike it rich.

The Silver Panic of 1893 had been hard on a lot of families. Silver mining had dried up in Leadville, Colorado, and those miners were looking for other jobs. With business now based on gold, rookie miners such as Papa, and seasoned miners, too, were all going to Cripple Creek to strike it rich.

Papa had regaled the family with wild stories of riches, found just under the ground, around Cripple Creek. He was not alone in this gold fever, Mary was sure. He had told her that there were now 13,000 people living within the mining area. The city of Cripple Creek alone had 6,000 people, along with hotels, newspapers, and railroads. Why there was even electricity and telephones in some places!

Papa contended that it was Colorado Springs' money that had sunk the first shafts and driven the first tunnels for gold. Villages had grown up around some of the big gold discoveries so that there were towns all up and down the mountainside: Anaconda, Altman, Victor, Gillett, Lawrence, Goldfield, and Elkton were some of their strange-sounding names. But Papa had decided that the big city of Cripple Creek was the place for him and his family — this was where he would make his money.

Secretly, Mary didn't think Mama was all that excited about this new-fangled idea of Papa's. She probably would have preferred to stay in Denver where there were familiar faces. It was true the Haskins didn't have the money that some of Mary's classmates had. Mary had to wear dresses Mama sewed for her and not the store-bought ones that some of her friends had. Having a store-bought dress had never been very important to Mary, anyway.

If it had been allowed, Mary would have preferred to wear the corduroys the boys wore. They seemed a lot more practical than those sissy long dresses and skirts. Every time she had asked her mother for a pair of trousers, Mama had gotten angry and declared that proper girls only wore dresses or skirts and shirtwaist blouses. Mary had finally given up in disgust. There was no way she was going to change Mama's mind.

Mary had heard some heated conversations in their Denver home when Papa was talking about joining the gold hunters in Cripple Creek. It had been the topic of conversation for more than a month. After Mary and Jacob had headed to the bedroom they shared, she would overhear the loud voices in the kitchen. Mary imagined Mama and Papa were sitting at the kitchen table with porcelain mugs of coffee between them, the words as heated as the steaming coffee. Sometimes the gold-camp conversations continued at the dinner table.

"Oh, Stephen, must we leave Denver? I just hate to think of leaving all our friends. Where will we shop and how will we live in that God-forsaken place with just old prospectors who don't know the first thing about civilization?"

"Now, Deborah, it's an opportunity of a lifetime, a chance to get the things we've always wanted. Oh, sure, it'll be hard going for a while, but when I strike it rich; we can come back to Denver and live in a bigger house with better furniture. We can travel, and the children can have fine educations."

Mama had pursed her lips in her don't-fool-with-me look, quickly turned around, and busied herself in the kitchen. Mary had watched the tenseness in her neck and shoulders as Mama worked. She hardly ever smiled anymore, but she seemed to realize there was no arguing with Papa once he had made up his mind.

So here they were, on the rutted path to Cripple Creek. The autumn in Colorado was something to behold. Dreamily, Mary watched the side of the road for the gold-brown-red scrub oaks, along with the green-gold mixture of the aspens and evergreens. Nature had provided its own set of jewels for her to enjoy as they bumped along. She even noticed a striped chipmunk dart across the road with a mouthful of dried grass. He was headed off to a nesting place for the winter, just like the Haskins family. Mary hoped they would have good luck with their move, just like the chipmunk seemed to be having with his winter home.

As they headed downhill into what looked like a gigantic volcanic crater, Jacob shouted, "There it is! There it is!" Mary's eyes shifted from daydreaming to the road ahead. She could see several mud-packed streets and dreary false-fronted stores with men in miner's gear strolling along the streets. Why, the sidewalks were only wooden boards! Where was the gold? Where were the glistening gems? Where was the city of Papa's dreams?

"Now, don't be disappointed, family." Papa had sensed everyone's feelings even though no one had spoken. Mary looked at Mama and saw the worry etched between her brows. Mary felt sick in her stomach because Denver was far away. They had traveled miles and miles over steep slopes and around narrow curves. It would certainly be different in Cripple Creek. How would the family ever learn to live in such a mud-spattered place?

Chapter 2
A CABIN IN CRIPPLE CREEK

Papa just kept that old buckboard headed up the muddy street and on up the hill. Suddenly he turned the buckboard to the right and up and up another hill until Mary could see a log cabin that looked deserted. The weeds were growing around it and the hinges on the door didn't hold it in place very well.

Mary glanced sideways and saw that her mother's mouth had dropped open several inches. "Stephen, this will never do. We can't bring children into such a house and expect to live here without any conveniences at all. Why, I bet there's even an outhouse in the backyard."

"Oh, Deborah, it'll be all right. Like I said, once you freshen it up a bit, it'll be our home."

Timidly, Mama, Mary, and Jacob walked inside to find one rickety wooden table in the middle of the room and old newspapers strewn all over. There were four chairs that looked every bit as homemade and dirty. Off to the back, Mary saw a room hidden by a curtain and guessed that was probably the bedroom.

In the corner was an old straw mattress that someone had left behind.

In the opposite corner, Mary noticed a home-made ladder that must be the passageway to an upstairs room. Mary guessed correctly that the upstairs attic room was Jacob's and hers.

"Where did you find such a place?" Mama wanted to know.

"Fella was moving out and offered it to me for next to nothing."

Mary glanced at Mama and knew Mama thought it was probably worth next to nothing.

"Look, family, I know this isn't the best of places, but we can fix it up, and Mama will add her special touches. It'll soon be a home we can be proud of. Besides, there are hundreds of miners sleeping on the floors of businesses down in Cripple Creek. You should be grateful I was able to find us a decent home with a roof over our heads. I even hear some of the men are dying from pneumonia because of the close quarters; so every one of you needs to understand this is just the way it's going to be."

With that remark, Mama shuddered at the thought of men actually losing their lives in order to strike it rich. She shrugged her shoulders in a wordless sign of resignation. There was no use arguing with Papa when he was so strong in his language. Even Mama knew better than to push the issue any further.

"Well, let's get busy." Mama took off her brown, thread-bare coat, tossed it onto the table, and opened one of the satchels that carried some of the necessities for getting the place in order. She pulled out a clean, crisp white apron and placed it resolutely over her head and tied it around her waist.

Even though the former owner hadn't been one for cleanliness, he had provided a wood-burning stove in the corner with a black pipe attached and running to the outside. There was also a sink with a pump that would bring water into the house for washing and drinking. But Mama had been right: There was an outhouse in the backyard. When Mary glanced out the back window, she saw the shed-like structure and shivered to think she would have to use that thing in the middle of the night if the call of nature came unexpectedly.

"Jacob and Mary, you all get changed and get busy helping." Mama always seemed to know just what to do. Mary was amazed at how she kept the family together. Mary and Jacob took a satchel up the stairs to the loft. She took off her traveling clothes and grabbed an old tattered brown dress and a smock to cover it. She kept on the same button shoes and black stockings. There were no others.

She helped Jacob out of his better trousers and into some old corduroys. They even had a patch in the knee. She rooted around in the satchel and found his old red-and-blue plaid shirt. It was Jacob's favorite because it was worn and comfortable, like an old friend he could trust in this strange country. Jacob looked up into Mary's eyes, grabbed her around the waist, and hugged hard. "Thanks, Mary." He put his hand in hers. They were ready.

As they backed down the steep stairs, Mary could hear Mama and Papa, busy in conversation. Somewhere Mama had found a dust cloth and was swiping at the table. One thing Mary hadn't noticed at first was that Papa had really prepared for their coming, because in the corner were several string bags of groceries. Mama brought one of the bags to the table and began to take out cans of food. Mary was sure Mama could make a tasty meal out of any old can of food. Mary noticed there wasn't any fresh food, like there'd been in Denver. Everything seemed to be in a can or bag.

Mary peered into one of the bags and found candy! Papa had brought a bag of licorice drops, those black candies that somehow stuck to the roof of her mouth with gooey sweetness and that always left a rim of black along her teeth and tongue.

"Papa, you remembered!" Mary had loved licorice since she'd been a small child. Now she knew it would be all right — any place that had licorice couldn't be all that bad. She popped one into her mouth and dropped one into Jacob's out-stretched hand.

"Mama, let me help you." She was in a better mood now that the licorice had sweetened things up a bit. She took the dust cloth and began cleaning off the chairs as Mama looked in her bag for a punch tool to open several cans.

Papa was busy carrying in some of the supplies they had brought from Denver. There was the Sunbonnet Sue quilt that had covered Mary's spindle bed — the little girl whose face could never be seen under her enormous bonnet was a part of home. Even as Papa walked to the back room with the quilt, Mary knew it would someday be keeping her warm in a real bed in the loft. Meanwhile, as Mama was tidying up the eating place for their first meal in Cripple Creek, there was a timid knock at the ramshackle door.

Mama wiped her hands nervously on her apron and opened it.

"Howdy, ma'am. My name's Samuel, but folks around here call me Old Sam." Before Mama stood a rough character dressed in dirty overalls and a collarless shirt with grimy stains all over it. "If you need any help, I'm just down the hill a bit. I saw your buckboard with the kiddies and thought you'd be settlin' in."

"Thanks, Mr. Samuel," Mama replied very properly. Mary watched and could see the tears begin to well up in Mama's eyes. Here she was in the middle of nowhere with no friends nearby, just a kindly neighbor who had offered to help.

"Ma'am, you seem a bit overwhelmed. Here, let me help!" Samuel limped by Mama and began to take over the chores of arranging some of the heavier furnishings so that Mama could busy herself with things in the corner where the kitchen was located.

Papa arrived at the door with another armful of possessions and spied the visitor. "Hello, I'm Stephen Haskins. Welcome to our new home!" He walked toward Samuel and vigorously shook hands with him.

Papa and Samuel continued to bring in the furnishings until Mary had to admit the combination kitchen-living room-dining room began to look lived in. Samuel helped Papa unload and arrange things, according to Mama's directions. Mama didn't want to seem ungrateful and had somehow found time to make a pot of bean soup while she was directing the moving in; so it was that Samuel joined the Haskins for their very first meal in a miner's house with barely enough provisions.

Samuel ate as if he hadn't had any home cooking for quite some time. Mama wrinkled her nose a bit when Samuel loudly slurped his soup from the spoon. He pulled off a piece of Mama's bread and

A miner's wife and children. If you use your imagination, it could be Mary and her family.
Denver Public Library, Western History Department, X-61353

stuffed it into his mouth, all the while keeping up a steady conversation.

"Tell me, Samuel, how in the world did Cripple Creek ever get its name? It sounds so strange. There must be a story behind such a moniker," laughed Pa.

"Well, it's true, Cripple Creek is an unusual name for a town. There're several stories floatin' 'round about, but the one I like best is about Bob Womack and an independent-minded cow.

"Seems old Bob was herdin' cattle for the Bennett and Myers Ranch 'round these parts when a stray cow took a mind to wander off from the herd down to a nearby creek. He followed with his horse fallin' into the creek and throwin' its rider. The cow broke her leg; the horse's leg and Bob's broke, too. It must have been a sorry sight! It seems as if everyone was crippled one way or another. That creek sure did cause a lot of bad luck, but the people hereabouts thought Cripple Creek was a better name for a rough-and-ready mining town than its earlier names of Fremont and Moreland. Sure does cause everyone to chuckle and makes for mighty interestin' conversations."

Mama gave him a prudish glare, but Papa burst out laughing. Mama shivered and passed another bowl of bean soup to Samuel.

Before too much longer, Mary and Jacob began to wrestle with trying to stay awake. The yawns began to come with increasing regularity until it was difficult to keep an eye open. Even though she was tired, as Mary thought about it, it had been a grand adventure so far. Climbing the ladder with Jacob close behind, she thought she might get used to Cripple Creek after all!

Chapter 3
FIRST DAY OF SCHOOL

The next day Mary opened her eyes and wondered where she was. The spindle bed had been replaced by blankets on the floor. Then she remembered the moving, the old-timer's stories, and their new home in Cripple Creek. She got up and donned her calico dress and smock. The black stockings and button-up shoes were a bit much, so she decided to go barefoot. She wondered if Mama would notice with all the work she had to do.

Mama was fixing porridge when Mary and Jacob arrived in the kitchen.

"It's time to think about school," Mama stated matter-of-factly.

Mary wished Mama wasn't such a firm believer in education, but it was always Mama's contention that schooling was what got people ahead in this world. Mary failed to understand how old arithmetic problems could make a difference, but she was too young to argue with Mama's stubbornness.

"There's a schoolhouse in town. You and I are going to meet the teacher this morning. We'll find out what supplies you'll need and when you can begin your studies."

After the dishes were cleared and Mama had Mary put shoes and stockings on her bare feet, the three of them descended the hill along the rutted road to town. As they approached the schoolhouse, they saw a square building with glass windows. It was much larger than Mary had thought it would be, but she was disappointed in its appearance.

Cripple Creek was growing so quickly that the building projects could hardly keep up. It was true that the town had five schools to accommodate all the new families; even though this school seemed to house all the grades, it was still smaller than the school Mary had attended in Denver — but at least it wouldn't be a one-room schoolhouse. She'd heard about those, and she certainly didn't want to be in a classroom with a first-grader — or, for that matter, a seventh-grader.

As Mama, Mary, and Jacob climbed the stairs, Mary noticed that the steps were beginning to show wear and tear from the constant tread of feet. A smiling woman dressed in a long black skirt with a crisp white shirtwaist stood at the top of the stairs and greeted them. Her hair was twisted into a bun at the back of her neck. Little wisps of brown hair had escaped from the bun and hung around her face.

"Hello, I'm Miss Jenkins. Welcome to our school! You must be new in town," she offered graciously.

"Yes, we are. We're the Haskins, and I'd like to register my little girl, Mary," said Mama primly.

"You'll need to go to the principal's office to fill out the forms, but I teach fifth grade, and I bet that's just the grade Mary will be in," Miss Jenkins said as she eyed Mary.

Mama strode into the main office, introduced herself, and began filling out the papers that would make Mary an official student in Cripple Creek. Miss Jenkins, who had followed them, led Mary back along the corridor and pointed to a shadowed, cool room, complete with wooden desks. There was an American flag to the right of the teacher's desk in front and a multi-colored map hung down behind the desk. The old pot-bellied stove stood in the corner and would, no doubt, be a welcome addition when the winter chill came to the mountains.

There were single desks and also double desks where two or more students sat, working on their arithmetic problems. The desks were dark wood with hard wooden seats that looked as if they could use pillows to make long hours of sitting more comfortable. There were two blackboards, one behind Miss Jenkins' desk and one on the side wall that contained a series of addition and subtraction problems. On the front blackboard the teacher had written a paragraph from a *McGuffey's Reader* for the students to copy and

A Denver classroom much like the one that Mary, Hannah, and Charles attended. Notice there are two students at some desks.

Colorado Historical Society, 10028813

correct. In the corner of the large front blackboard was a list of ten spelling words that Mary thought she would have no trouble with when it came time for Friday's test.

Mary had loved spelling bees back in Denver. Students would line up on either side of the room and try to spell words given out by the teacher. Very often Mary would be one of the last students standing. Words such as *audacious*, *officious*, and *separate* were fun to spell because the words just seemed to roll off the tongue. Besides, when Mary had to use the words in sentences, it made her sound so smart!

As Mary gazed around the room, all the children were sitting at their desks, pretending to be immersed in their studies, but she could see several pairs of eyes peering at her. The children were all different sizes; one girl, glancing from under long eyelashes, caught Mary's attention. She was dressed in a blue-flowered calico dress with a white-ruffled long smock. Her hair was pulled back in pigtails and tied with blue ribbons. Mary thought she was the prettiest girl she'd ever seen. The calico-dressed girl returned Mary's stare with a timid smile.

Mary's attention slid to the quirky, mischievous smile of a boy sitting behind the pretty girl. He looked up to no good, and Mary decided she would avoid him if at all possible.

Meanwhile, Mama was talking to Miss Jenkins in muted tones about the expectations of the school, the grade that Mary had completed in Denver, and the necessary supplies Mary would need to bring tomorrow. Miss Jenkins said, "Mary can stay here for the day. I'm sure we can find some writing paper and pencils for her."

She assigned Mary to a desk across the aisle from the pretty girl with pigtails, who whispered, "My name's Hannah. Take some of my paper and here's an extra pencil for your lessons."

Mary nervously thanked her and began copying the ciphers on the side blackboard. When she glanced up from her paper, she realized Mama and Jacob had left. Miss Jenkins was sitting behind her desk, marking papers. Suddenly Mary felt very much alone.

Chapter 4

LUNCHTIME

The clock on the side wall indicated noon, and Miss Jenkins rose from her chair. "Children, it's time for lunch. Line up and get your lunch buckets from the coat-rack shelf."

The children obediently walked to the back of the room, took down their lunches, and waited in line for Miss Jenkins to dismiss them. Mary's mouth dropped open when she realized she had no lunch. In all the rush to get to school, Mama had forgotten it.

Mary was standing behind Hannah as the kids rushed out to the playground for lunch and games. Mary sat quietly under the one shady tree in the schoolyard. Hannah noticed and came hesitantly to sit next to her.

"You can have half my cheese sandwich," Hannah said. Mary knew in her heart that Hannah's gift was almost more than she could bear. Food was often hard to come by in Cripple Creek because produce and canned goods had to be hauled all the way from Colorado Springs or Denver. Tentatively, Mary took the sandwich and whispered a thanks that made Hannah's shy smile light up her entire face.

"Is your Papa working in the mines?" Mary asked.

"He's one of the shift superintendents," Hannah offered proudly.

"Gee, you must be rich." Mary realized that Hannah's family could well afford several cheese sandwiches for miners' children.

"We live way up the hill in a white two-story house, but I don't think we're that rich." Hannah certainly wasn't going to be a snobbish classmate. Mary remembered her rich friends in Denver and how they had made the poorer children feel so bad with their uppity ways.

As lunch progressed, the talk was about Cripple Creek and all the new immigrants coming in daily to strike it rich. Just as lunch time came to a close, that mischievous imp who sat behind Hannah came up to the two girls and pulled one of Hannah's pigtails again. "Gotcha!" he yelled. Hannah winced and said, "Don't pay any attention to Charles Watkins. He's always looking for attention. He always manages to get Miss Jenkins' attention, that's for sure."

Mary couldn't help but think Hannah was much too kind to old Charley. She'd have given him a trip with an extended foot or at least said something mean to him, but not Hannah.

As the bell rang announcing the end of lunch, Mary felt as if she had a new friend. When Hannah took her hand and swung it back and forth, Mary was sure of it.

Chapter 5
SETTLING INTO GOLD-TOWN LIFE

P apa entered the door after his first day in the mines. His face was a black mask of dust, his shoulders were hunched over, and he sank, rather than sat, in a chair. Mary could see Mama's concerned look as she brought a cup of hot coffee and a biscuit to the table.

"Thank you," was in Papa's look, but the effort to speak was too much.

As he sipped his coffee and chewed on his biscuit, Mama kept up some idle chatter. "Stephen, you'll never guess what I did today. We finally have clean windows and pictures on the wall. Why I even fixed the hinges on the front door," Mama boasted proudly.

Papa glanced around the room with a weary smile. "That's good, Deborah. My day was really hard, but one of these days, my muscles will toughen up. I'll get the hang of this gold mining soon."

Mama busied herself at the stove and soon sounds of spoons hitting pans filled the kitchen. Mary began setting the table, giving Papa a wide berth as if his soot and tiredness would rub off on her.

Papa rose slowly from the table and washed his face and hands with soap at the kitchen sink. As he washed, Mary noticed his shoulders straighten and his body take on a more rested stance. It was just as if the water had magic powers to make Papa all right again. Mary sighed with relief: Papa would be fine. It would just take him a while to get into the swing of things. Just like she had to adjust to school with new friends and new studies, Papa would have to learn to adjust to the hard physical labor of working down in the mines.

Mary kept thinking about Papa and the mines as she set the table and helped Mama with the dinner preparations. Papa had sat back down at the table and was reading *The Cripple Creek Times* newspaper. Someone must have left it at work because Mary knew Papa wouldn't have spent the money to buy a newspaper. The family's money was much too precious to spend on that.

"Look here, Mama!" Papa exclaimed, *The Times* says there's a smallpox epidemic going on in Denver! There must have been a good reason for us to leave and just in the nick of time, I'd say," boasted Papa.

After Jacob came in from the front yard, they sat down at the table and bowed their heads. As Papa said grace, Mary took a quick glance at him and saw that the tiredness had truly begun to leave his face. That old gold mining must be mighty hard work, especially because he had not worked with his hands in Denver. Mining would take some getting used to.

Chapter 6
MEETING MR. STRATTON

It was Saturday, a day of freedom. Mary wondered, "Why am I standing here washing dishes?" Dreamily, she gazed out the window and thought about all the events that had happened this week: the arrival in Cripple Creek; meeting Old Sam, the crusty prospector with a kind heart; and, most of all, school, where she had met Hannah.

Suddenly Mama broke into her daydreams, "Okay, okay, get going. I can't stand your slow ways." Mary's daydreaming stopped immediately. She wiped her hands on a ragged towel and, with a quick "Thanks, Mama," she rushed out the door and up the hill to Hannah's house.

The homes became bigger and more elaborate as Mary headed toward Hannah's. The best were the farthest from the bustling town.

Hannah was sitting on her front steps, head in hands, looking glumly at the ground. She glanced up to see Mary approaching and a smile lit up her face.

"I thought it was going to be a boring Saturday. Mama's off to a quilting party, and Papa's in town. Now I know it'll be a good day because you're here!"

Mary beamed inside with Hannah's praise. "It was true," thought Mary. "I'm good at thinking of interesting things to do."

"Let's go down to town," squealed Mary.

"Oh, dear, I'm not sure Mama would approve," Hannah said.

But Mary saw that Hannah was wavering. The thought of fun was too much for shy little Hannah.

"I'll beat you down the hill," Mary said breathlessly as she took off. Hannah, much more calmly, followed in Mary's footsteps until both of them stood on Bennett Avenue.

They heard the sidewalk boards creaking underneath their feet as they strolled the town. Down the street underneath the First National Bank sign, Mary spied a white-haired, mustachioed gentleman surrounded by a group of well-dressed men.

"Who's that?" whispered Mary. "He looks like some sort of important person."

"Don't you know? That's Winfield Scott Stratton, the richest man in three states," replied Hannah. "He discovered lots of gold at the Independence Mine up there on Battle Mountain. He's rich, rich, rich." Hannah pointed upward toward the mysterious mountain that held all of Mr. Stratton's riches.

As the girls approached him, Mary let her gaze settle on this handsome, upright man. His pale blue eyes caught Mary's stare, and he smiled and lit up with a gleam of mischief. "He looks like a kind man," thought Mary.

As they came closer, Mary saw that Mr. Stratton had two silver dollars in his outstretched hand. He flipped one coin toward Mary and another toward Hannah. Both girls grabbed at the coins. "Thanks, sir!" they said in the same breath.

Mary looked down at the shiny silver dollar. She thought of all the things one dollar would buy — unlimited amounts of candy at one of the town's general stores and maybe a new smock for her blue calico dress. Her mind wandered through all her dreams.

If she went to the general store, Mary knew she would find all kinds of wonders to tempt her. She decided to buy just a bag of licorice and save the rest of her money for later. Just like Mama and Papa, she would be thrifty and put the change in a box in her dresser drawer.

"He really is a kind man," Mary stated as she fingered the coin while visions of gooey licorice filled her thoughts. She and Hannah smiled at each other, and Mary could tell Hannah was thinking about how to spend her riches, too.

Skipping away down the street, Mary and Hannah entered the Palace Drug Store and glanced at all the treasures on the shelves and behind the wooden counters. There were sewing articles that would entice Mama. There was medicine for everything from rheumatism to liver ailments, but she and Hannah headed right to the candy counter with its bright colors and tempting flavors. They looked at each other, smiled, and

Winfield Scott Stratton, the owner of the Independence Mine.
Colorado Historical Society, F-2458

put their orders in to Mr. Gordon, who was standing behind the counter with a wide smile on his face. Mary supposed he was used to breathless children coming in with their pennies, looking for their favorite candies. Hannah decided on the glistening rock candy that was so hard it made one's teeth hurt. But Mary, true to her word, ordered a bag of licorice. Then the two friends skipped out of the store and silently thanked the kindly Mr. Stratton, who had provided them with such great fun.

Chapter 7
STRATTON AND THE INDEPENDENCE MINE

On one of Mary's free days she decided to see the old prospector, Sam, who had helped them move into their cabin. She was really interested in finding out more about Winfield Stratton, the generous man who had provided her with money for candy.

As she approached the cabin down the way, she saw Old Sam perched on his front steps with an unlit pipe in his mouth, just gazing off into the distance and listening for the mine whistles that signified a shift change. "He must be missing all the excitement of gold mining," thought Mary.

"Mr. Sam, I came to visit!" shouted Mary before Sam even saw her coming.

"Why, hello, young lady! What's new with you and your family?"

"I think we're settled in, at least for the time being. My family really thinks it was a good thing you did, helping us move in. We couldn't have done it without you."

"It was my pleasure. I'm always glad for the company. Now that I don't get up to the mines, I'm pretty well stuck here by myself. It's always good to see friendly faces. One of these days I'm plannin' to come over to your place and see if there's any fixin' up that needs doin'."

"I know Mama and Papa would appreciate that, because Papa's so busy in the mine these days," said Mary. "But I wanted to ask you something about Mr. Stratton. My friend Hannah and I saw him in town the other day, and he gave each of us a silver dollar. I know he's rich because of his old gold mine."

Mary saw Old Sam look across the rutted path, and he seemed miles away as he started to tell his story about Winfield S. Stratton. That's what Mary liked most about Sam — his stories.

"It seems old Stratton staked his gold claim on the Fourth of July, you know, and that's why he called his mine the Independence. Seemed kinda the natural thing to do. Anyway, Stratton was just an old carpenter in Colorado Springs when he went prospectin' for gold hereabouts after talkin' to that old geezer, Bob Womack, about his gold discovery. Womack showed him some land, but Stratton wasn't satisfied — no, siree.

"It's true that Stratton had been a Colorado Springs carpenter durin' most of the year, but in the summers he'd prospect all up and down these mountains. I heard he'd also studied geology and metallurgy at Colorado College in Colorado Springs, so he knew enough to look for gold on Battle Mountain — up there. And Old Sam pointed in the general direction of the mountain peak where Stratton had struck it rich.

"He saw a great outcroppin' of granite, a sure sign of gold — take that advice from this old prospector. He didn't find that gold right away, but he thought on it awhile and, sure o'nuf, that varmint found what he was lookin' for — the mother lode, a real jackpot, for sure! For awhile he only dug out the gold he needed. I guess he figured it was safer in the ground than in a bunch of bags, strapped to a burro. That gold would be mighty temptin' to any old thief who came down the pike."

Sam paused to take a breath and light up his pipe. Mary waited as patiently as she could, but Old Sam's story was telling just like a mystery-thriller.

"He took his first bunch of gold to Guyot's Assay Office. Lo and behold, it was worth $380 a ton! That Stratton was the luckiest devil I ever laid eyes on! You know he's our first millionaire in these here parts. Why, he's the King of Cripple Creek. Now everyone thinks he can strike it rich, just like Stratton.

"He's a nice gent, though. Like you said, he'll give you money just for fun, or if a fella's down on his luck, he can count on Stratton to help out. I heard tell he's given money to the Salvation Army, down-on-their-luck miners, and lots of other needy folk. Now that he's moved back to Colorado Springs, we don't see him quite so often up here.

Guards at W.S. Stratton's Independence Mine.
Colorado Historical Society, F-33,743

"I wouldn't be surprised if he up and sold his Independence Mine one of these days, and it'll fetch him a lot of money, for sure. Word 'round town is that he's gettin' bored with all that money and can't figure out what to do with it. Sounds like a problem I'd like to have," chuckled Sam.

Mary thought how pleased Papa would be to be able to trade places with Mr. Stratton. Papa's eyes always got twinkly when he talked about staking a claim for a mine one of these days. First, he'd have to make a lot more money.

Mary guessed Stratton was really well liked and not just because he was rich, but because he was so kind hearted and generous. She felt a little sad for him, though, because, even though he had a lot of money, he didn't have a wife or children. Mary could imagine that he must be lonely. Maybe that was the reason he had menfolk around him all the time. He needed someone to listen to him.

Chapter 8
THE GREAT CRIPPLE CREEK FIRE

Mary would never forget April 25, 1896. She awoke that morning with an acrid smell in her nose. Sleepily, she walked to the loft window, looked out toward the town and noticed smoke rising from Myers Avenue. Then the sound of six shots rang out, the signal that there was a fire.

Mary yelled down the stairs, "Mama, Mama, what's happening?"

Mama came to the bottom of the stairs, "It's a fire in town. Hurry up and get dressed! We have to go to town to help!"

Mary shook Jacob awake and dressed him quickly as he rubbed the sleep out of his eyes. Jacob sat on the edge of his bed as Mary jumped into her clothes, ran a brush through her hair, tied a ribbon around it, and put on her button-up shoes. Together, the pair backed down the steep stairs to the kitchen below.

Mama had laid out a bowl of oatmeal along with a pitcher of milk. Mary plopped down on a chair, grabbed her spoon, and gulped down the porridge until her stomach rumbled in protest. Jacob played with his oatmeal, now eating a bite, now pushing it around the bowl. Jacob was usually a good eater. Mary figured he was just being ornery because Mama and she were in such a hurry.

Finally Mary grabbed Jacob's hand as she and Mama hurried out the door. Mama carried a huge bag full of food and bandages. When they reached town, Mary saw people scrambling around in panic, screaming. Everything was in disarray. Mary stared dumbfounded at the chaos before her. She could feel her stomach tense and the hairs on the back of her neck rub against her dress. The sweat was beginning to dampen the palms of her hands. This was a Cripple Creek she had never seen before.

Mama, holding Jacob's hand, trudged down Bennett Avenue, jostled by people moving wildly in all directions. The mine alarms were screeching their warnings. Mary held onto the back of Mama's dress for fear they would get separated. She might never see Mama again! Mary's thoughts ran wild just like the people who surrounded them.

Mama marched as proudly and purposefully as she could with the care bag clutched tightly in her right hand, the hand of her squirming son in her left, and a frightened daughter tugging on her from behind. She reached the Portland Hotel and hurriedly walked inside with the children in tow. Mary peeked from behind Mama, let her dress go, and straightened her shoulders as she took a step toward Mama's side. Jacob found a small friend, Teddy Gordon, in the corner of the hotel lobby and ran excitedly to him. Teddy was the young son of the drug-store owner who had waited on Hannah and Mary not too long ago. The boys busily amused themselves with a stuffed bear Teddy had brought with him.

As she gazed at the hotel lobby's wide expanse, Mary saw men sitting sadly in chairs, arms hanging between their legs, just staring at the floor. Some had sooty faces and arms, water-spattered work pants, and muddy shoes. Mary even noticed some women amongst the men who were wringing their hands in despair. One woman had stray hairs winding around her face as if she had forgotten to clean up and brush her hair properly before leaving the house.

Mama was a take-charge lady. Hadn't she nursed several Denver families through their bouts with smallpox? Now it was time to put Cripple Creek back to order! There were other women, Teddy's mama included, who were helping the frightened crowd with food and aid. Mama joined the women. "Mary, help me!" she demanded.

Mary snapped to attention and grabbed a proffered napkin filled with buttered biscuits to pass out to the nearby people. As she passed out the food, Mary noticed the grateful glances. She knew in her heart that food would not solve the problem of the fire's aftermath, but just knowing that others cared seemed to make a difference with the fire survivors.

Meanwhile, Mama and some of the other women were ministering to those people who had been wounded by the fire's flames and the falling timbers with bandages, salve, and iodine. It was as if the women were Florence Nightingales. Just like the Crimean War nurse who had cared for the wounded soldiers, they were helping the fire-ravaged folks. There were looks of gratitude in the men's eyes, as if the women were indeed angels of mercy.

Outside, the volunteer firemen, including many miners, were rushing around with their horse-drawn hose carts, trying desperately to put out the flames that licked around the wooden buildings. The men had even enlisted the help of the stubborn burros that seemed to run the town on most days. It was a useless activity, because the fire had gotten such a head start.

But even if one building could be saved, it would be worth all the effort.

Mary and Mama, along with the other women from Cripple Creek, continued to serve the wounded and hungry. As the day wore on, Mary's feet would hardly walk one in front of the other. She thought she just might keel over from fatigue. But she looked at Mama making her rounds, and decided she could be just as brave.

The miners came from all around the area to lend a hand. Word had spread that the Portland was the center of activity, and that a group of women there was healing the wounded and feeding the needy. As a group of miners entered the hotel, Mary saw Papa. He looked tired and dirty, but it was Papa, and he was safe!

"Papa, Papa, we're over here!" yelled Mary at the top of her lungs. Papa glanced around and caught her eye. He edged his way through the crowd and grabbed Mary around her waist and swung her in the air.

"Thank goodness, you're safe! We heard the alarms ring, saw the smoke in town, and came running. I didn't have a chance to see if you and Mama and Jacob were all right."

Mary pointed to Mama who was putting a bandage around a man's scratched arm. "Deborah, you're okay!" Papa called above the bedlam. Mama turned and gave him a weary smile. She and Papa met somewhere in the middle of the hotel lobby, embraced, and whispered to each other. Mary guessed they were just glad to see each other.

"What about Jacob?" Mary heard Papa ask. Mary had forgotten all about the little tyke, and Mama certainly wouldn't know. Mary looked around the room, desperate to find her brother. Suddenly, all three pairs of eyes spied Jacob and his friend asleep in the corner of the room. It was amazing to Mary that he could sleep amid all this chaos. Maybe his early wakening this morning had been the reason he could fall asleep so completely with such commotion all around.

Mama scurried over to Jacob, lifted him into her arms, and returned to Papa's side. Mary and Papa held hands, and the four of them headed for the door. As Mary glanced back at Jacob's friend, she saw that he had begun to stir and that Mrs. Gordon had reached down to take his hand.

It had been an unbelievable day. Mary was tired, but the Haskins family was together.

Mary later heard Papa reading aloud from *The Denver Republican* newspaper that was circulating among the townsfolk:

> *"Jennie Laurie had a quarrel with her boyfriend. A gasoline stove was turned over. One-third of Cripple Creek was destroyed; one million dollars' worth of property was burned and 3,000 people rendered homeless. Buildings destroyed included the post office with 25,000 undelivered letters, the First National Bank with the jail and town hall, the Gold Mining Stock Exchange and*

The Cripple Creek fire of April, 1896.
Colorado Historical Society, F-2193

a hundred stores, saloons and offices and 300 dwellings of all classes with 90% of their contents — in less than three hours' time."

The town had just settled down and begun to clean up when a second fire broke out on April 29, 1896 — a cold and windy day. The reservoirs were dry from the first fire, so there was no water to fight this one, which had broken out in the Portland Hotel's kitchen. The flames went from there to the Winsor and Palace Hotels, a fire so hot that 700 pounds of dynamite exploded in a nearby store. Again, *The Denver Republican* reported the devastating news:

"Last Saturday's horrors were repeated three-fold in the destruction of the portion of Cripple Creek left by the first disaster by a second fire this afternoon. To an increase in the amount of property destroyed on Saturday, the fire today adds the loss of life and leaves from 3,000 to 4,000 people home-less...The business portion of the city left standing tonight is less than what would cover a city block...The town is out of bread."

By the next day, the train whistles announced incoming help for the homeless Cripple Creek people. Mary and Hannah rushed down to the train depot. They watched as huge bundles of foodstuffs — sacks of flour and beef halves — were delivered to their fire-ravaged city. Two Santa Fe baggage cars held provisions including bedding, clothing, and cooking utensils.

"I can't believe people in Denver are so kind and care about us so," Hannah offered.

"I saw everyone helping at the Portland last Saturday, so I know there is more kindness than we can imagine," said Mary. "Why I even heard our friend, Mr. Stratton, contributed blankets and tents to help out those people who lost their homes."

Mary was sad about the Portland Hotel being burned during the second fire. Right where she and Mama had been working had been completely destroyed, nothing but rubble and dust to testify to its ever having existed. In fact, the only structure left standing on Bennett Avenue was the G. W. Gardner Building.

Mary's attention and thoughts were drawn back to the train depot and the bustling men unloading the much-needed food and equipment. They grabbed their handkerchiefs out of their back pockets to wipe off the sweat gathering around their hat brims.

By the Saturday following the first fire, the Denver Relief Committee was on duty in Cripple Creek, helping the homeless in make-shift tents and shelters. It wasn't long before Governor McIntire and Adjutant General C. M. Moses arrived on the scene to survey the damage. Both of them left, shaking their heads in wonder that so many people had survived the catastrophe.

Mayor Steele, along with some other influential men in the community, decided that there would be no more shack building out of wood and other combustible materials. From now on Cripple Creek would be a city of stone and brick. The Portland was rebuilt, much to Mary's delight, along with the Palace, Winsor, and the National Hotels, and the First National Bank.

The saddest thing to Mary was not just that so many people were homeless, but that hoodlums had looted some of the businesses and threatened to use dynamite if the merchants didn't cooperate with their demands. Luckily, an emergency squad of townsfolk caught the culprits and locked them in a bull pen. "Good punishment for the scoundrels," she decided.

Every time Mary looked down on the city of Cripple Creek from her loft window, a great sadness would take hold of her. She watched the men of the town begin to rebuild in brick and stone. One building after another arose out of the ashes. Mary gathered strength and hope, watching all the work. The town had even formed the Sheltering Arms Society as an aid to those people who were left homeless. The money would help families put their lives and homes back together again.

Even with all the hustle and bustle of rebuilding a town, Mary still worried about her family's house. Would it, too, go up in flames? There wasn't enough money to build a new home out of brick. For now, Mary decided that she was just glad that the worst seemed to be over. Maybe everything could go back to Cripple-Creek normal once again.

Chapter 9
A BURRO RIDE

It wasn't long before the fires seemed like a terrible memory that would never happen again. It was May and then June, and before Mary could finish up with her studies, it was the last day of school. She and Hannah had a whole summer to play and explore the area in and around Cripple Creek!

As soon as Mary could be released from her household chores, she raced up to Hannah's home. Mary was always thinking of ways to have fun. She thought it wasn't that she was a mischief-maker, but that trouble always seemed to find her.

They could run wild on the hills above Cripple Creek or play hide-and-seek or tag, but those games all needed more children than just Hannah and Mary. Of course, they could always play ladylike activities such as jump rope or jacks, but she was not one to sit around just doing proper young-lady things.

Mary's mind was reeling from all the planning. It was just a day of fun with her best friend, but, even so, she had one great idea that she hoped she could convince Hannah to do. When she arrived, breathless, at Hannah's home, she yelled, "Hannah, Hannah, let's go into Cripple Creek! I have a great idea for a good time!"

Hannah peered around the front door and looked just a little bit skeptical. "What's your idea?" she asked cautiously.

"You know those burros that are always wandering around town? Well, let's have a ride!"

"What are you talking about?"

"Just what I said. Let's go for a ride on one of the burros. We could grab him by the scruff of his neck, climb aboard, and ride around town for all we're worth!"

Hannah's eyes began to gleam as the idea took hold. "Just a minute while I tell Mama we're going down to town. I won't mention what we're going to do down there."

Hannah and Mary held hands as they skipped into town, sure that this would be a day to remember. As they meandered along the street, skipping dirt clods and dodging horse-drawn wagons, they spied a lonely burro standing between two newly built brick structures. The girls walked on tiptoes so as not to disturb the burro's daydreaming.

Suddenly Mary grabbed the burro by the scruff of the neck while he whinnied in fright. He was an ebony, bristle-furred creature with ears that pointed skyward. Around both eyes were rings of white, and he had a white blaze on his chest. As Mary climbed up, she thought he was a handsome animal. Most people laughed at their slow ways, but the miners had depended on these sturdy creatures for many years.

Children riding burros, much like Mary and Hannah.
Colorado Historical Society, 10028808

They made dependable pack animals to and from the mines, and they provided companionship for the lonely prospector. They ate grass and twigs so their upkeep was minimal, and they could climb over rocks and rough terrain with nary a whimper. He really was the miner's best friend, but somehow they had run wild in the streets of Cripple Creek. Maybe they came from miners who had abandoned their gold-mining dreams. Sometimes after a lot of hard work and no gold, the men would give up their mining stakes and return home, leaving their burros behind.

Now Cripple Creek was home to these orphaned animals that had been so hard working and loyal. Many locals would feed them leftover food, and they would often forage around town on anything that was available.

For now, the one burro that had the unfortunate luck to be in the wrong place at the wrong time was the object of Mary and Hannah's giggles as they hiked up their dresses and clumsily climbed up on the burro's broad back. He tensed and stood still until Mary gave him a gentle kick in the ribs. It was then that they had to hold on for dear life.

Hannah was hanging onto Mary's waist and Mary was holding onto the burro's neck as he sped from between the buildings and down Bennett Avenue. Mary noticed that people on the sidewalks were watching in wild-eyed amusement. She even saw one woman put her hand over her mouth to cover an unladylike snicker.

Mary and Hannah began shrieking at the tops of their lungs. The burro's lopsided gait made Mary move from side to side in a most unpleasant way, but because neither she nor Hannah had a rope tied around the burro's neck, there was no way to stop his frightened gallop. Racing down Bennett Avenue at such a fast pace caused Mary to get dizzy from the whirling colors and objects.

Hannah, in a frightened voice, screamed, "Stop him, Mary! Stop him!"

"I can't! I don't think this was such a good idea!"

As the burro neared the top of Bennett Avenue close to the train depot, all the commotion, with people running after them, must have caused the burro to think he wanted to end this wild ride, too. He straightened his legs, stopped in his tracks, and didn't budge. Unfortunately, Mary and Hannah didn't stop quite as quickly; and they fell from the burro and into the mud. Mary saw stars swimming in front of her eyes, but not so many that she couldn't see Hannah having trouble rising from the ground.

When Mary had regained her senses, she yelled, "Are you okay, Hannah?"

"I think so. I'm really not sure. Ask me again in a few minutes!"

As Mary looked around her, she saw that a crowd had gathered. Some of the men were guffawing at the adventure-turned-dangerous. Some of the women showed a real concern for the girls' condition.

"Let me help you up, young lady," proffered a well-meaning gentleman. Several others reached for Hannah, as well. When they were both on their feet and brushing off the dirt and mud from their dresses, Mary noticed that the well-meaning gentleman was Mr. Stratton! He winked at her and strode off into the crowd. This was the second time she had met him face to face, and it was the second time he had done something special for Hannah and her.

Hannah sniffed and walked, straight-legged, along the street. Mary could tell she was angry. "This is the very last time I listen to your hare-brained ideas, Mary Haskins!" she snorted.

Mary smiled to herself, because she knew she could still sweet talk Hannah into any adventure that came along.

Chapter 10
THE FOURTH OF JULY PARADE

As the Fourth of July approached, Mary began to hear more and more about the special celebration that was being planned. The town officials wanted people to have some fun and get out of the funk that everyone felt after the devastation of the fires in April.

Christmas, New Year's, and even Easter often came when the weather was at its worst. In Colorado snow and cold could come at any time of the fall, winter, or spring. In fact in March and April, when many other states were getting their spring showers and flowers, Cripple Creek was usually getting snow. Mary really didn't mind, because there were always snow fights and snowmen and snow forts, not to mention sledding, to help keep up everyone's spirits.

On July 4, 1896, Mary awoke with a niggling thought in her mind. Something special was going to happen. Then, as the sleep left her eyes and body, she remembered. Today was the big Fourth of July celebration! She rushed to dress and backed down the stairs, two at a time. As she looked out the window, she could see the sky was an iridescent blue, with puffy clouds and a bit of wind ruffling the grasses along the path.

"Mama, Mama! It's the day of the big celebration!"

"I know, silly. We'll finish up our work here and head down to town." Mary thought Mama sounded just as excited as she felt. It was sure to be a good time.

"We've just got to get to town before the parade begins," whined Mary. She was ready to see and hear all the festivities and music.

Jacob came into the kitchen, rubbing his eyes and climbing onto one of the chairs at the kitchen table. Papa moved the curtain separating the living area from the bedroom. The family was together. There was no work today for Papa: It was one of the few days off in his work year. Mary's eyes twinkled. She could hardly wait for the day to begin!

She raced around straightening the kitchen and washing and drying the dishes. Meanwhile, Mama was busy with a basket hamper, making a picnic lunch that the family would enjoy after the festivities in town. There was a small can of milk and several sandwiches with Mama's homemade bread. She even remembered to put in a few licorice drops for Mary and Jacob.

Mary watched as patiently as she could, first standing on one foot and then the other. For the longest time, Mama and Papa dawdled around doing unimportant things, or so it seemed to Mary.

"Mama, may I go up and get Hannah? I promised her she could go with us to town."

"Make it snappy!" Papa said.

Mary sped up the hill toward Hannah's house and saw her, too, waiting impatiently at the front door. "I thought you'd never come. What took you so long?"

"Oh, you know grownups. They always find something to do when there's fun to be had. But we're ready now. Mama's packed a lunch and the whole family is ready to head down the hill. Let's go!"

Just as Mary and Hannah arrived at the Haskins' home, Mama, with Jacob in tow, and Papa, with the picnic basket over his arm, were just leaving the house. The four-Haskins-plus-one trooped down the hill to Cripple Creek. As they traveled the rutted road, Papa kept arching his neck up and over the womenfolk to see if he could find a good place for all the festivities.

Mary looked down and saw crowds of people already gathered for the parade and races. Where in the world would there ever be a place for them? Suddenly a gruff, gravelly voice called out, "Stephen, over here!"

It was one of Papa's miner friends. He had saved a few spaces at the edge of the street. He and Papa must have made this arrangement ahead of time, knowing that the streets would be crowded with merrymakers, parade participants, and onlookers.

"Thanks, John. Family, this is John Basker. He and I work together in the mine." The group smiled politely and stood where Mr. Basker indicated. As Papa and Mr. Basker began talking about mining, Mary's attention was drawn to hilly Bennett Avenue. She could see wagons of some of the fraternal organizations with all those funny-sounding names such as Odd Fellows, Brotherhood of Elks, Fraternal Order of Eagles, and the Woodmen of the World lining up with their members wearing neatly pressed, soldier-like uniforms with gold epaulettes on their shoulders.

From someone's trumpet came the signal to begin. Why, Mr. Stratton was at the head of the parade! He was the grand marshal!

The parade finally began. Women and men were draped in red, white, and blue ribbons and bunting. The horses, mules, and burros were even decked out in

Fourth of July splendor. Mary noticed one burro with white rings around his eyes and a blaze on his chest. She wondered if this was the very same burro that had caused so much mischief for Hannah and her. No, it couldn't be — or could it?

Next, the local band of amateur musicians from the mines and schools marched down the street with brass instruments that glistened in the sun. Mary noticed an array of trumpets, drums, and trombones. Oh, it was grand! She could feel her feet twitching as if they just wanted to get up and jump around. Even little Jacob was bouncing up and down to the loud music. He just couldn't settle down.

Before Mary could grab his hand, Jacob was off and running toward the band. She gasped and glanced quickly at Mama, whose attention was on Papa and Mr. Basker. Without so much as a good-bye, Mary was off and running after Jacob. He dived between the musicians and was zigzagging from one to another. Mary couldn't decide what to do: She daren't interrupt the musicians' playing or marching. Soon she caught sight of Jacob's towhead ahead of her. He jumped in front of the marchers. Because Mary was older and faster, she ran to the front and grabbed him by the arm, dragging him away from the musicians' marching feet.

"You little dickens! Mama will have our hides!" shouted Mary. Jacob looked rather crestfallen, but Mary could see there was a twinkle in his eye as he glanced up toward her sheepishly. "Now let's go, and be quick about it!" Mary decided that she must be the strict older sister, or Jacob never would realize he had almost gotten them both injured. Mary began to soften just a bit as their footsteps took them closer to Mama and Papa. Hadn't Mary been the one to jump astride that burro just a few days ago? But she wasn't about to let Jacob off without a talking to.

"Mary, where have you and Jacob been?" queried Mama as they trudged up to the group.

"It's okay, Mama! I found him trying to play in the marching band!"

Mama grabbed Jacob by the hand and didn't let go. Mary breathed a sigh of relief as she thought about what could have happened if she hadn't reacted so quickly. Now that Mama was completely in charge of Jacob, Mary could watch the rest of the parade.

There was the Fraternal Order of Eagles, men dressed in elegant uniforms with sabers, bright cummerbunds, and all kinds of colorful decorations on the fronts of their uniforms. They all marched stiff and straight, right down Bennett Avenue.

Next came the ladies of the Sheltering Arms Society that had played such a large part in finding food and lodging for the victims of the horrible fires last spring. Mama even waved to a couple of the women who were marching in line. Mary remembered how she and Mama had helped during the first fire. She crossed her fingers behind her back and hoped that there would be no more fires in Cripple Creek.

After the parade was over, Mary and her family hiked up a hill, looking for a grassy knoll where Mama could spread out the tablecloth for a picnic. Mary, Hannah, and Jacob raced ahead and found a spot with a small shade tree to sit under. Mama proceeded to shake out the tablecloth and put out bowls of fried chicken, baked beans, apples, and milk. Mary munched her food. She and Hannah lay back on the cool grass and searched for cloud shapes in the blue sky.

"Oh, there's an elephant," squealed Hannah. "And there's a butterfly."

Mary's eyes began to get heavy, and Hannah's voice drifted off. Before she knew it, Mama was shaking her shoulder.

"Mary, wake up! It's time to head back to the house."

Sleepily, Mary got up, skipped ahead with Papa, and headed for home. Wasn't it the best Fourth of July she'd ever had? Where could she have found all the glitter and excitement that this parade had offered?

Chapter 11

LEARNING ABOUT
CRIPPLE CREEK TRAINS

Ever since Mary and Hannah had watched the unloading of the trains after the fires, Mary had wanted to revisit the train station to watch the puffing locomotives lumber into town. There was something fascinating about the loud noises and smoky steam that entranced her.

So it was that one summer day Mary found herself wandering down to the new Midland Terminal Depot to watch the passengers unloading and loading from the Colorado Springs and Cripple Creek District Railroad cars. It was a standard-gauge railroad track, four feet, eight and one-half inches wide. Mary had already learned there were also narrow-gauge railroad tracks — three feet wide — in Colorado because many trains had to maneuver narrow chasms with steep cliffs on one side and sharply steep mountains on the other. It was a treacherous journey, and the engineer was a man of many talents to guide that awkward train around the bends and twists that led from Cripple Creek to Colorado Springs.

She was watching intently as the Colorado Springs/Cripple Creek Railroad, with a deafening screech of brakes, stopped directly in front of her. Alighting from the train was a host of men, women, and children dressed in their Sunday best and looking for familiar faces among those people waiting at the depot.

There was a gentleman in a brown wool suit with a watch fob dangling from his vest pocket. He looked quite prosperous. Although he was unfamiliar to her, Mary wondered if he was a merchant in town. There were many men who had come to take advantage of all the gold being mined. To Mary, it seemed as if the really wealthy people in town were the merchants, not the miners.

Many of the businessmen had grubstaked some of the early miners, and they were the ones who reaped the money when a discovery was made. The only person Mary knew who had mined and made his millions was Winfield Scott Stratton, the man who always seemed to be saving her from imminent disaster.

As her mind came back to the scene at hand, Mary noticed the brakeman was directing the hookup of another car to the already long train. Perhaps there would be a lot of passengers for the next trip to Colorado Springs. It was the big city that always beckoned people down from the mountainside. As far as Mary was concerned, she'd had enough of cities when she'd lived in Denver. She much preferred the bustling town of Cripple Creek.

The brakeman motioned to the engineer who, in turn, eased the train slowly backward toward the lone car. It looked as if the brakeman and engineer were involved with a huge jigsaw puzzle. Oops, no, not this time. The brakeman pushed his hand forward, indicating to the engineer to pull forward once again.

Slowly, the engineer repeated the process of easing the train back toward the lone car. With a smile of satisfaction, the brakeman held up his thumb and index finger in a round O to indicate a perfect hitch. The brakeman seemed to be an expert in what he did, and the engineer seemed pleased with himself as well.

Mary's attention now focused on the engineer, sooty and sweaty, as he hopped from the engine cab. He wiped the moisture from his brow with a handkerchief he grabbed from the rear pocket of his overalls. He glanced up and saw Mary watching his every move.

"Well, missy, what's new in Cripple Creek these days?"

Mary's mouth dropped open as she mumbled, "Nothing much. That's a fine-looking train. Could I see what it looks like inside?"

"Why, sure. Hop up!"

Mary grabbed his outstretched hand as he climbed back up the steps to the front car. She stared at all the dials, but what really caught her attention was the cord hanging down from the middle of the cab ceiling. The engineer watched as he saw the look of puzzlement on Mary's face.

"Would you like to see what that cord's for?"

"Sure," Mary stated firmly.

The engineer lifted her up toward the cord, and her hand grasped the rope. She pulled and soon was covering her ears! The noise it made was loud and strident. The engineer laughed a belly laugh as he set Mary down on the cab floor.

"Guess you didn't know that cord's attached to the whistle."

Mary managed to laugh at the joke, but her ears were still ringing as she thanked the engineer a bit shakily and jumped off the step to the station platform. She glanced toward the front of the engine and noticed a pointed iron attachment on its front. She yelled up to the engineer, "Say, mister, what exactly is that contraption on the front of the train?"

"Why that's called a cowcatcher! It's a pretty strange name unless you want to catch some cows with this big train," the engineer laughed uproariously at his joke. Mary thought he was certainly having a good time at her expense, but she persisted.

"What's it used for?"

"It's really used to remove rocks or anything else that falls into the path of this mechanical monster. We can't just stop for every little thing that stands on the tracks, so we use this giant scoop to shove things out of the way. What's even more amazing is, in the winter, we attach a huge snowplow in place of the cowcatcher so that we can have an automatic scoop for the snow that piles up in these parts. The snow always seems to land smack dab right on the tracks during some of our heavy snowfalls. Just wait and see how ferocious winter can be here. Last winter was pretty mild; just wait till a whopper comes along!"

Mary was deep in thought about what the engineer had told her. As she walked toward the back of the train, she noticed the conductor on the platform. It must be a while before the next train leaves, Mary surmised.

"Would you mind if I got on board to see the inside of the train?" she queried.

He pulled his railroad pocket watch from his vest to double-check the time. It was shiny gold with

The Cripple Creek Short Line, one of the trains that carried goods and people to and from Cripple Creek. Colorado Historical Society, 10031256

a chain attached —quite elegant, or so Mary thought. These trainmen certainly were sticklers for being on time.

After confirming that there was time before the next trainload of passengers arrived, he said, "Sure thing! I'll give you the grand tour myself, young lady."

As Mary followed the conductor up the steps and onto the metal platform that separated two train cars, she glanced into the car on the right-hand side. What she saw made her wish deep inside that she, too, could ride in one of these trains someday. As the conductor led her into the car, Mary could see the plush red velvet upholstery and the glistening wood armrests. Toward the front of the car, she noticed the all-too-familiar spittoon that held tobacco residue from the men's chewing tobacco. Mary's nose twitched at the stench that came from the brass receptacle. If she ever rode in a train, she would be sure to sit as far away as possible from that filthy spittoon.

The conductor strode down the aisle, absent mindedly gathering up odds and ends of trash that people had left. But Mary's attention was drawn to the plush seats and the wide windows that surely would offer a fast-moving view from the train. The blinds would help when it came time to sleep or when the sun was too bright. All together, Mary thought the train was the most amazing machine she'd ever seen. It certainly beat that old mule-driven buckboard her family had arrived in.

As the conductor reached the back door of the car, Mary said, "Thanks for the tour. Some day I want to ride on a train. It looks like a lot of fun."

"It surely is a comfortable ride, compared to the old buckboards and horses; but come prepared with card games and a good book because time can hang heavy on your hands. Of course, you can always take a nap or watch the world go by outside your window."

As Mary alit from the train car, she noticed a long, hooked pipe coming around from the water tower. "They must be getting ready to take on some water," thought Mary. "Using all that steam up and down the mountainside must surely make it necessary to take on water at regular intervals."

The pipe, attached to the side of the tower, was positioned over the train's engine room. The water gurgled down inside the train's water container. The fireman who had managed to accomplish the transfer of water pulled the chain that replaced the water pipe back against the side of the tower, ready for the next train.

One other stop Mary wanted to make was the red caboose that always sat so jauntily at the end of the train. She thought it would be fun to wave at the trainmen riding in that last car. Someone had said it was good luck if they waved back at you.

As Mary approached the squared-off caboose, she spotted a trainman stepping down from the stairs. "Could I please see the inside of the caboose? I'm on an adventure to learn everything I can about trains," Mary asked politely.

"I don't see why not," he replied as he gave her a lift up the steps and into the narrow passageway at the back of the caboose. On either side were cabinets that must have supplies stored inside. Mary knew that when the trainmen weren't on duty, they could rest and relax in the caboose.

She walked out of the narrow hallway into the caboose, noticing an area to her left that contained a table and two benches. This must be the place where the men ate, played cards, or read during their time off. There was a small pot-bellied stove across from the table so that the men could warm themselves in the cold of winter.

As she stepped down the caboose steps, she waved to the trainman. "Thanks for the tour." Mary hoped someday she'd be able to ride the rails, just like all those folks she'd seen get off the train earlier.

Chapter 12

THE FLIM-FLAM MAN

S lowly but surely, Papa had managed to gain strength from his work in the mine. He had come home less tired, and he even playfully wrestled with Jacob on the floor. The work seemed to be agreeing with him because his arms were now muscular, even if they were dirty most of the time.

One evening Mama was humming "There'll Be a Hot Time in the Old Town Tonight," which had been playing around Cripple Creek lately. Mary was surprised that straight-laced Mama would hum a dance-hall tune. Supposedly it had originated in Cripple Creek, and everyone was singing or humming along. Mary much preferred the short song:

> *Goin' up to Cripple Creek*
> *Goin' on the run,*
> *Goin' up to Cripple Creek,*
> *To have a little fun!*

Tonight Papa was late from work. He was always home just when the old cuckoo clock chimed six. It wasn't like him to miss Mama's dinner that she put on the table promptly at 6:05.

"It looks like something's delayed Papa. You children go ahead with dinner while I clean up the kitchen a bit."

Mama's worried frown was contagious. Mary could feel her stomach tighten up. She hoped there hadn't been a mining accident. She hoped Papa was all right.

Of course, Jacob sat on the stack of books that brought his chair up to the edge of the table and eagerly gobbled down some potatoes. Mary had never known Jacob to pass up dinner. His stomach was just like a mule's — it always needed filling. Because Jacob was so busy eating, he seemed unaware of the worried looks that passed between Mary and Mama.

Mary pushed her food around on the plate and constantly looked at the clock. Mama always said a watched pot never boiled, but she couldn't take her eyes off the wall where the clock hung. The bird on the cuckoo clock sang out seven warbles, and Papa still wasn't home. At seven-fifteen Papa entered the door, tossed his miner's hat on the kitchen table, grabbed Mama around the waist, and swung her off her feet.

"Deborah, you'll never guess what happened today!" Before Mama could catch her breath, Papa continued, "A man stopped by the mine as we were all getting off work, telling us about a new mining find further up the mountain. He was going on and on about the riches to be made. You know that's what we came to Cripple Creek to find — more money for a better way of life. Why he even showed us some of the ore from the mine and took us up the mountainside to see the mine for ourselves. There were gold nuggets lying on the ground, just there for the picking! I don't think they'll even have to dig below ground, or if they do, it looks like it'll be a rich vein, just like the one Stratton found at the Independence.

"I know I make about three dollars a day at the mine, and I'm not sneezing at that; but I want my family to live better than a miner's family. I want my children to have the things we never had. Wouldn't it be great to see Jacob go on to college and become a doctor or a lawyer? Wouldn't it be wonderful if Mary could have some of those fancy dresses we used to see down in Denver?"

Mama glanced up at Papa with one of her don't-fool-with-me looks, but it was hard for her to argue with Papa about the riches he wanted for the family.

Mama wanted the same things; she was just more practical about how they got them.

Mary knew there would be a lot of talk tonight. Mama and Papa always made decisions together, even though it was always Papa who had the final say. Mary remembered the nightly discussions about moving to Cripple Creek when Mama and Papa had thought she was asleep. Now Papa wanted to buy shares in this mine. Mama was sure to have a fit because she was the one who always managed the family's finances. Papa might be the one who brought the money home, but it was Mama who rationed out the dollar bills. She just had a better head for figures, and Mary knew Mama could save the dollars as quickly as a cat could wink.

"Now Stephen, hold on! We need to talk. This is a pretty risky business you're getting us into. Remember, we have two children to care for. Coming to Cripple Creek is one thing, investing in a mine is another."

"But Deborah, the fellow says if every man contributes just a little bit, we'll all be rich. Those nuggets were beauties! He said there were more where those came from. All the fellows are going home to find a little extra money that's been tucked away."

"If this mine's so rich, why's he sharing his wealth with the whole community?" Mama queried.

"Apparently he doesn't have much money himself, and he can only afford the equipment and supplies. Just consider this a grubstake, Deborah! I know several men who've become wealthy just by buying into a mine. Don't you think it's our turn to take some of my salary and put it back into a going venture?"

Mama still looked skeptical, but she knew it was a lost cause, trying to convince Papa that this was a risky adventure. He had really made up his mind before he'd come home. It was as if Papa had changed and was a different person. Mary hated it when he got the gold-fever look in his eye. Right now he was more interested in the gold than he was in little Jacob who tugged at his work pants, wanting Papa to play.

"We're going to need to get to the bank tomorrow and draw out some of our savings. Basker and Old Sam down the hill aways both say they're in as partners, too."

As Mama put the chicken and vegetables on the table for Papa and herself, Mary could see that

Mama's shoulders were hunched over. Mary knew Mama was disappointed. It was going to be just like the time Papa had decided to move to Cripple Creek. There would be tortured silences as Mama went about her business around the house, only speaking when spoken to, especially with Papa. Mary dreaded the thought of sadness in the house once more.

"It'll be okay, Deborah. You just wait and see. We'll have more money than we know what to do with. Who knows, I might even get rid of these dirty old miner's clothes and open up a shop in town. We could live in the back of the store. Mary could have a new piano. Jacob could have some fine clothes."

Papa was always the dreamer, but it was Mama who kept the house running. Mary wished that both of them could be happy about this decision.

"Papa, I'd like to visit where you work. Now that summer is coming to an end, I want to squeeze in every last bit of fun before I have to study all the time," Mary begged her father.

"You know, I think that might be a dandy idea. You know the mining supervisor won't let you come down into the mine, but I could show you the bucket we go down in and introduce you 'round to all my friends."

It was decided that Mary would go to the mine with Papa that very next day. She rose early when she heard Mama and Papa rustling around in the kitchen below. Dressing quickly so as not to disturb Jacob, Mary jumped down the ladder, two rungs at a time. She was getting to be quite the sprinter on that old ladder!

"Are you ready, Papa?"

"Whoa, wait a minute, young lady. You'll not leave this house without a good breakfast," Mama said. "There she goes again," thought Mary wearily. "Another meal of oatmeal and milk."

Mary sat down resignedly, knowing she would have to endure the torture of waiting to leave until she'd gulped down the lumpy stuff. She quickly finished, grabbed her coat from the rack beside the door, and rushed for Papa's hand as he was kissing Mama goodbye. They were off.

Papa carried his tin lunch bucket in which Mama had, no doubt, put a pasty, often called the "miner's food" because it was a meal in a biscuit. Mama would roll out the yeast dough and fill it with cabbage, meat, onion, and any other vegetables she could find. She would seal the ends of the dough with a bit of water on her fingers so that the food inside couldn't seep out, and then she'd bake it in the wood-burning stove. Mary loved these closed sandwiches and often asked for them as a special treat for Jacob and her.

Papa would also have a tin full of milk and maybe a pastry that Mama had lovingly baked. Because the miners worked so hard, they could be mighty hungry when the noon lunch whistle sounded.

Papa also carried his soft-sided miner's hat, which was meant to protect him from falling rocks. Mary'd heard the mine could be a dangerous place. There could be a build-up of gas, or a rock could drop unexpectedly from the actions of pick axes or dynamite, which loosened the gold from the ore veins deep underground. Mary tried not to think too much about all the dangers Papa faced each day. She preferred to think about the happiness he must have felt when he came home with his paycheck and knew the family was provided for. It was important for Papa to get ahead so that the family would have more luxuries. Mary trudged next to him as he strode assuredly toward the rail line that would take them to the Mollie Kathleen Mine. She had to take two steps for every one of his, so that she felt sure she was running or skipping and not just walking. Papa seemed to be in another world as he hurried along the path toward town. Mary knew he was thinking about the mining investment he was about to make. She could practically see the gold shining in his eyes!

They headed to the steam railway to catch a ride up the hillside to the mine. As they gathered at the stop, other miners soon joined them, and before long Papa was engaged in earnest conversation.

"Well, what do you think about that offer yesterday, Stephen?" asked John Basker, the miner friend Mary had met at the July Fourth celebration.

"I'm inclined to give it a try. I can't see making our fortune working for another man, like Mr. Stratton or Mr. and Mrs.Gortner, the Mollie Kathleen owners. Why they're getting rich from all our hard work! It's about time the wealth was passed around a bit, don't you think?"

All the way to the mine, all Mary heard was how everyone would soon be so rich, and they'd have a house-building boom in Cripple Creek or maybe even in Colorado Springs. As they alit from

the railway car at the mine, there was a man in a
gray tweed suit, watch fob at the waist, waiting for
them. He had a big handle-bar mustache and an
oily way of grinning. Mary didn't like the looks of
him, but his appearance didn't seem to bother the
miners one bit.

"Well, fellas, what did you all decide? Is the
mine a go? What about all of us becoming rich?"

"I'm in!" replied Papa, and several others sec-
onded his opinion. The tweed-suited man was now
grinning like a bear who'd found a honey tree.

"Okay, then, let's meet down at the bank right
after that old end-of-work whistle sounds. See you
down in town tonight."

"It was a done deal," Mary thought. She could
just imagine Mama's look when Papa told her about
drawing out all their savings to place in the hands
of a man they didn't even know. Things moved
mighty fast in Cripple Creek, Mary guessed.

After the business deal was struck, Papa
returned to his usual kindness and introduced Mary
all around. "This here's my little girl. She's all
excited about visiting the mine. Can't say I blame
her! This is the place to be," he chuckled. "Why if

she could, she'd go down in the mine, and she'd get all sooty and sweaty, just like us."

The men laughed, scooped up their lunches, and headed for the mine bucket. They stepped inside and grabbed the hoisting cable that would jerkily carry them down into the darkness. As they began their long descent, Papa yelled from the bucket, "Mary, you know you'll need to take the railway back to town." He threw out several coins for her to catch. She decided she'd be glad when all this hoopla was over with and Papa was back to normal again. He could hardly think of anything else except gold these days.

It wasn't long before Papa had a chance to think about something else besides gold. The scuttlebutt around town began about a week after the miners had given the fast-talking man their money: He had skipped town, along with their investments.

When Papa came home with the news, Mama had a didn't-I-tell-you-so look. She pursed her lips, as if willing them to stay shut: She knew Papa would not take kindly to being reminded that there had been cooler heads in the house the night he'd decided to sink their savings into a mining venture.

Apparently, or so the talk went, the man had been a scoundrel of the worst kind. He had preyed on the miners' desires for riches and had salted an area in the Anaconda Mining District. He'd thrown around enough gold nuggets so that the miners would think there were plenty more just for the taking. None of the investors had bothered to have the mine checked out properly. It didn't help Papa very much to know that there'd been others who'd fallen for the smooth talker's honeyed phrases. Mary could tell, by his sheepish look, that he was mighty embarrassed when he delivered the news to Mama.

Of course, the sheriff had alerted the Colorado Springs and Denver police forces to let them know about the scam. They might find him, or he could very well be on his way to St. Louis or Chicago or New York City.

Papa apologized over dinner. "Look, family, I'm sorry about taking our savings. Now we'll have to start all over again."

Neither Mama nor Mary could fault him when he had such a depressed look on his face. "It'll be okay, Stephen," Mama said. "I still have money stashed away in the coffee can over the sink. We can manage until the next paycheck. I'm beginning to think three dollars a day sounds mighty good."

Papa smiled and silently thanked Mama for being such a good sport. He'd learned his lesson, even if it had been a painful one. "Never again," Papa promised. "Never again will I listen to an old flim-flam man."

Chapter 13

PANNING FOR GOLD

Papa continued his daily trek to the mine, but Mary could tell he was still worrying about all the family's money he'd lost in the mining scam. There wasn't a thing that Mary could do, or so she thought.

One day she was listening to one of Old Sam's stories. This time it was Mary's turn to stare off into space as Sam rattled on about his adventures.

"Why I remember pannin' for gold in that old Cripple Creek that caused Bob Womack so much trouble. I was swirlin' that sand around in the metal pan. Lo and behold, I found a shiny nugget starin' me in the face! It was the dangest thing you ever saw — a shiny piece of gold! I could already hear the money janglin' in my pocket."

All of a sudden, Mary's attention was drawn to the last phrase, "money janglin' in my pocket." That was it! She could help out the family after all. She could get a pan and start mining for the surface nuggets that must be lying near Cripple Creek. If it had worked for Bob Womack and Old Sam, it could work for her and her family.

She jumped up, spoke a quick thank you, and said goodbye.

"Hey, missy, where're you goin'?" yelled Sam.

"I'm off to discover gold!"

Mary rushed into the family's log cabin and headed for the ladder leading to her loft bedroom. Mama was busy in the kitchen making biscuits for dinner.

"What in the world are you doing, Mary?"

"I think I know how we can get more money. Trust me, Mama!"

She clambered up the steps and headed for her dresser. She opened the top drawer and drew out a box. She peeked inside and found the coins she'd gotten in change from Mr. Stratton's silver dollar. Thank goodness she had decided to save some of her money! She grabbed the coins, slipped them into her pocket, and climbed backward down the ladder.

"I'll be home before dinner, Mama."

Mama shook her head and continued with her baking.

Mary skipped down the path toward town and entered the hardware store. "Do you have any gold pans for sale?" she asked.

"Why sure we do, young lady, but what's a young thing like you going to do with a gold pan?"

"I'm going to pan for gold so my family can have some money," remarked Mary proudly.

"Well, don't be surprised if you don't find anything. I think the creeks around here have just about given up all their riches," the clerk informed her.

Nevertheless, Mary put down her coins, grabbed the pan from the clerk, and headed out the door humming: "Goin' up to Cripple Creek/Goin' on the run,/ Goin' up to Cripple Creek,/ To have a little fun!" As she glanced at the gold pan, she realized it looked a lot like her mother's pie pan. The only differences were that this pan was made out of a heavier metal, was bigger, and had deeper sides. Mary decided it should be able to do the job, all right.

She walked through town and up to the creek. Amid the overhanging brush and willow trees, Mary glimpsed the creek. She noticed it was flowing south, so she went north, toward the source: She'd heard the headwaters might contain some valuable nuggets.

At a place where the creek slowed down a bit, Mary stopped, took off her shoes and socks, hiked up her dress, and put the hem under her belt. Mama would have a fit if she ruined one of her dresses, even if it was an everyday one.

Bending down on her knees, she noticed the shiny black sand near the creek bank. Papa had said that black sand was the best indication that gold might be found nearby. Old Sam had once shown

Mary and her family lived in a log cabin very similar to this one.

Mary how he'd panned for gold in the old days. Following his directions, she took the pan, swishing it through the water and filling it with sand, gravel, and water. By swishing the water around and dipping the pan toward the creek, she slowly rid it of water and lighter material. Mary's knees and back began to ache as she continued swirling the water until just the black sand was left. She looked closely and could see no gold dust — and certainly not any nuggets.

Again and again, Mary dipped her pan, picking up gravel, sand, and water, until finally she was rewarded with a few grains of gold. She carefully picked out the small pieces and put them in a hand-kerchief she carried in her dress pocket.

Mary continued to visit the creek every chance she got. Several times she even found small nuggets, as well as gold dust. Every time she would carefully carry the grains and nuggets home and put them in her box in the dresser.

Chapter 14
A FAMILY IN CRIPPLE CREEK

Ever since Papa had lost the family money in the salted-mine deal, he had been silent and withdrawn. To Mama's credit she had not kept reminding him of his mistake. Mama was always one to let bygones be bygones.

Nevertheless, Papa couldn't seem to get over his depression. Even Old Sam, who often wandered over for dinner, couldn't seem to shake Papa's gloom.

"Oh, Stephen, you know you aren't the first one to fall prey to those scoundrels. There's always someone ready to make a buck out of someone else's misery. They seem to know when a fella wants to get ahead and has the gleam of money in his eyes. I know I once wanted to strike it rich. The luck just never seemed to go my way," offered Sam sympathetically.

"Why look at you. You've got a fine wife and good, decent children to come home to after a hard day's work in the mines. I gave all that up for the gold curse. That's just what it is, too, a curse! I think we men sometimes get so caught up in lookin' for the almighty quick dollar that we forget what's really important."

Papa gave Sam a pat on the back and a weak smile in response, but Mary could tell Sam's wise words weren't registering with Papa. Sam leaned back in the kitchen chair and gazed off into the distance, just as Mary had seen him do while talking about Mr. Stratton. It was clear that Sam was no longer in the Haskins' home but in another time and place.

In his imagination he was probably, once again, trekking the Colorado mountains with his gray-muzzled burro. The pack animal would probably be loaded with a pick axe, shovel, and other mining tools. Some local merchant had probably grubstaked him; that way, if Sam struck it rich, the storekeeper would see part of the profits from Sam's venture. No doubt, he'd also been carrying some flour and coffee, maybe sugar, dried meat, and oats for his burro — just the bare essentials for living in the wild.

"It must have been a lonely experience," thought Mary. "Maybe that's why Sam nowadays likes to talk and tell his tales to anyone who'll listen. He must have missed having people around in those old prospecting days." Mary felt a shiver run down her spine and realized she had been daydreaming, too.

"I'd better be gettin' back home. It's gettin' late." Sam broke the special silence that engulfed the small kitchen.

After Sam left, Papa put his feet up on Sam's abandoned chair and leaned back in a relaxed manner. Mama put a cup of hot coffee in front of him and a mug of steamed milk in front of Mary. She brought a cup of coffee for herself, sat down at the table, and joined the twosome.

"This has certainly been an interesting year," admitted Mama. This was quite a confession, because Mama had been the one family member who hadn't wanted to come to Cripple Creek. Even little Jacob had been excited about the new adventure. For sure, Mary and Papa had thought Cripple Creek would be much more exciting than Denver with its civilized culture.

"Papa, I have a surprise for you!" Mary said.

She ran to the ladder and climbed up into the loft. She opened her dresser drawer and took out the box that contained the gold nuggets and dust that she had worked so hard to find. She placed the box in her pocket and climbed down to the kitchen.

"Close your eyes, Papa," she ordered mysteriously. He smiled just a little and shut his eyes. "Hold out your hand."

Papa held out his hand, and Mary placed the box in it. As he opened the box, he also opened his mouth in surprise. "Wherever did you get this gold, Mary?"

"I've been panning! You've been looking for a big strike like Mr. Stratton, but I decided a lot of little strikes might add up."

"Mary, that was a thoughtful thing to do," Mama said. Papa's eyes were shiny, and he grabbed Mary's arms and lifted her into his lap. He gave her a kiss on the forehead.

"I think there's so much gold in Cripple Creek that we might be able to find some more. Maybe we could even pan for gold as a family," he said.

"That's exactly what we have become — a family," thought Mary.

She looked at Papa, and for the first time in a long while, he was smiling.

ACTIVITY PAGE

1. Find ten words in the story that you do not know. Look up the definitions and put the words and their definitions in alphabetical order.

2. Choose something you learned about mining or about Cripple Creek. Write a story about it. Several suggestions might be: the life of a burro in Cripple Creek, going down into a mine, or taking a train ride to Colorado Springs. Don't forget to use colorful words to describe the experience. You want your reader to be able to picture what is happening.

3. Imagine going to school in an old schoolhouse. Write about your experience or draw a picture of your classroom.

4. Winfield Scott Stratton was an interesting man and is honored in Colorado Springs for all the good things he did. Find out more information about him. Where will you look?

5. Write a sequel to the story. What happens to Mary after the story ends?

6. Draw a map of Cripple Creek along Bennett Avenue. What were some of the businesses that might have been there? Remember some of the stores in the story.

7. If you had lived in Cripple Creek during 1895-96, what would be some of the activities you would have enjoyed? (Remember: The children did not have television or radio to entertain them.) Write a description about one of your activities.

8. Find out about other mining towns in Colorado, such as Leadville, Creede, Ouray, Silverton, and Telluride. How were they different? How were they the same?

9. Colorado is a state with such an interesting history. There were many people who lived and visited in Colorado. Find out about one of them and write a short story about your person. Suggestions might be Theodore Roosevelt, Ulysses S. Grant, Jefferson Randolph Smith, Doc Holliday, Horace Tabor, Isabella Bird, or Katharine Bates.

10. Draw a picture of what a miner might have looked like when he was ready to go down into a mine. What would he need? Look at one of the pictures this story to get some ideas.